Casper the Kid Cowboy loved
his horse more than anything
else. Blue was always loyal
and friendly.

They went *everywhere* together.

To the park . . .

To the shops . . .

6

This book belongs to:

....

....

For Alex
C.C.

For my beautiful little moo,
Natasha Kitty, with love xxx
J.McC.

Reading Consultant: Prue Goodwin, Lecturer in literacy and children's books

ORCHARD BOOKS
338 Euston Road, London NW1 3BH
Orchard Books Australia
Hachette Children's Books
Level 17/207 Kent Street, Sydney NSW 2000

First published in 2011 by Orchard Books
First paperback publication in 2012

Text © Catherine Coe 2011
Illustrations © Jan McCafferty 2011

ISBN 978 1 40830 685 7 (hardback)
ISBN 978 1 40830 693 2 (paperback)

1 3 5 7 9 10 8 6 4 2 (hardback)
1 3 5 7 9 10 8 6 4 2 (paperback)

Printed in China

Orchard Books is a division of Hachette Children's Books,
an Hachette UK company.

www.hachette.co.uk

Horse Horror

Written by
Catherine Coe

Illustrated by
Jan McCafferty

ORCHARD

Sometimes even to bed . . .

Casper's best friend, Pete, usually came along too. His horse was called Funny Fool. Pete loved Funny Fool, but sometimes he had a mind of his own.

Whoa there! Stop, boy!

Casper and Pete agreed that
everything was more fun with
their horses.

Today, Casper and Pete were planning a day out. They had packed a tasty picnic.

The two cowboys were looking forward to having fun riding across the desert plains.

But Casper's horse wouldn't
move.

"What's the matter, Blue?"
Casper asked. It seemed
his horse didn't want to go
anywhere today.

"We'll have to go without him," Pete decided. "It's OK, partner. You can ride up here with me."

Casper was sad. It wouldn't be fun without Blue!

"Let's go this way," Casper said.
"No, let's go that way!" Pete
replied.
Funny Fool was confused!

At last the cowboys agreed
to ride west. But Funny Fool
didn't want to go that way.
Instead, he set off towards the
mountains in the east.

"Whoa there!" Pete said to his horse.
But Funny Fool had made up his mind. He galloped . . . and galloped . . . and galloped . . .

Soon they were at the top of
a mountain!

"If Blue was here, I don't think
we would have gone the wrong
way," Casper said. He sighed.
"Let's eat our picnic."

But Casper didn't feel very hungry.

Pete didn't want to eat much either. He was afraid of heights!

It was lucky that the two cowboys weren't hungry. Before they could start eating, Funny Fool had stolen their lunch!

Then they heard a rumbling
noise. Casper realised there was
a storm coming. Soon it was
pouring with rain!

"Can we go home now?" said Pete, shivering.

"Yes, please!" Casper cried.

He was desperate to see Blue. It hadn't been any fun without him! The soggy friends jumped onto Funny Fool.

Home, boy!

But Pete's horse wasn't ready to
go home. He wouldn't move!
There was nothing else for it.
Casper jumped off
and pushed.

Finally, they arrived at Casper's ranch. Pete ran over to Blue. He still looked unhappy. "What's wrong with him?" Casper asked his best friend.

"Maybe he's tired?" Pete
wondered. But Blue didn't
look tired. "Cold?" Pete guessed.
But Blue didn't look cold.

"Why don't you examine him?"
Pete said. "Start at the bottom."

Very slowly, Casper moved
towards Blue's bottom.

"Not *that* bottom!" Pete laughed.
"At the bottom – his feet!"

Casper moved away from Blue's bottom *very* quickly. He looked at his hooves instead.

"You're right!" Casper said. Blue's hooves looked sore and swollen.

He needs new horseshoes!

As soon as Blue had new
shoes, he was like a new horse.
It was amazing.

"Yee-ha!" the cowboys shouted,
as Blue trotted round and
round. Casper's horse looked
so happy!

As the sun set, Pete smiled at his best friend. He had been silly to think they could have fun without Blue.

And having fun was what they
did best!

Written by **Illustrated by**
Catherine Coe **Jan McCafferty**

All priced at £4.99

Orchard Books are available from all good bookshops,
or can be ordered from our website: www.orchardbooks.co.uk,
or telephone 01235 827702, or fax 01235 827703.

Prices and availability are subject to change.